DAMIAN DROOTH
SUPERSLEUTH

SPYCATCHER

Other books by Barbara Mitchelhill

The 'Eric' series:
Eric and the Striped Horror
Eric and the Wishing Stone
Eric and the Pimple Potion
Eric and the Green-Eyed God
Eric and the Voice of Doom
Eric and the Old Fossil

The 'Damian Drooth, Supersleuth' series:
The Case of the Disappearing Daughter
The Case of the Pop Star's Wedding
How to be a Detective

The Great Blackpool Sneezing Attack
Kids on the Run

DAMIAN DROOTH
SUPERSLEUTH

SPYCATCHER

BARBARA MITCHELHILL

Illustrated by TONY ROSS

Andersen Press • London

For Rachel with love

First published in 2006 by
Andersen Press Limited,
20 Vauxhall Bridge Road, London SW1V 2SA
www.andersenpress.co.uk

Reprinted 2007

Text © 2006 Barbara Mitchelhill
Illustrations © 2006 Tony Ross

The rights of Barbara Mitchelhill and Tony Ross to be
identified as the author and illustrator of this work
have been asserted by them in accordance with the
Copyright, Designs and Patents Act, 1988.

British Library Cataloguing in Publication Data
available
ISBN 978 1 84270 567 4

Phototypeset by Intype Libra Ltd
Printed in the UK by CPI Bookmarque, Croydon, CR0 4TD

Chapter 1

I expect you know my name. Damian Drooth, Supersleuth and Ace Detective. I've solved loads of crimes – but there was one mega case which stands out. It involved big business, money and lies and was dead exciting.

It started one Saturday morning. The kids had met in my garden shed as usual for the Detective School – Winston, Harry, Tod and his kid sister, Lavender. I gave them tips on how to solve crimes for a fee of only one packet of crisps (which I think is very reasonable).

That Saturday, Lavender was looking fed up, which wasn't like her. Her mouth was all droopy and she wasn't listening to my instructions on how to track criminals through a crowded shop. All the others were really interested. But not Lavender.

'You look a right misery, Lavender. What's up?' I asked.

For some reason, she burst into tears and all the lads turned round to look at her.

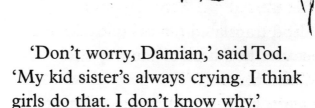

'Don't worry, Damian,' said Tod. 'My kid sister's always crying. I think girls do that. I don't know why.'

We tried to carry on with that morning's lesson as best we could but Lavender was making so much noise we found it hard to concentrate. When the howling got too loud, we had to give up.

'Right,' said Tod, coming face to face with his sister. 'Tell us what's wrong or I'll take you back home.'

She shut up then and sniffled a bit and managed to say, 'It'th Mr Thwan. He'th in tewible twouble.'

'Mr Swan?' I asked. 'Who's he when he's at home?'

'Mr Thwan is a vewy old man who livth by himthelf.'

Sometimes it's hard to understand what Lavender says. But you have to be patient and listen. She's only a kid after all.

Tod translated for the rest of us because he's used to the way she speaks. She was talking about Mr Swan who lived in Water Lane next door to Tod's gran. Lavender and Tod often went round to see the old man, who usually talked to them and let them play in the garden. He didn't mind them playing football because his garden was a bit overgrown.

'He'th uthually ever tho kind. He
givth uth owinge jooth and bithkits,'
she said.

'So you get orange juice and
biscuits,' I said. 'What's the problem?'

'No owinge jooth. No bithkits. Now
he gets vewy angwy. He shouts at uth.
He'th weely thtwange.'

'So suddenly he's become strange,
eh? Mmmm. Something must have
happened. But I wonder what.'

'He won't tell uth,' said Lavender.
'It'th a mythterwy.'

A mystery, eh? Not for long, if I had anything to do with it. Something spooky had happened to Mr Swan – like in that film 'Dr Jekyll and Mr Hyde' where he drinks some potion that makes him change into a monster. Just give me time and I'd get to the bottom of it.

Chapter 2

I amazed the kids by working out a plan of action right there and then.

'You're bwilliant, Damian. You fink of evewyfink,' said Lavender.

We disguised ourselves as gardeners (complete with gardening tools) and left the shed without Mum spotting us.

We headed for Water Lane and, when we got there, Lavender and Tod went to their gran's house to keep her out of the way. I went and knocked on Mr Swan's front door with Winston and Harry standing behind me on the path.

After a while, Mr Swan unbolted the door and opened it – but only a fraction.

'Who are you?' he said in a crackly voice. 'What do you want?'

Lavender was right. He was dead old and very odd.

'We are the Help-the-Pensioners Team of the Boy Scouts,' I said, 'and we have come to do your garden.'

(Tod had told me that it was a bit untidy. It needed loads of weeding and stuff.) But Mr Swan wasn't having any. 'Clear off!' he said and was about to slam the door when I jammed my spade into the gap.

'We are here to help,' I said, giving him one of my famous smiles. 'The vicar sent us.'

'The vicar?'

This was a lie but I was sure the vicar would approve.

'Well . . .'

'There's no charge. We will do your weeding for free.'

Lavender had told us he was poor so I knew I was onto a good thing.

'Is that so?' he said. 'I suppose it would be all right. You could trim some of the bushes too.'

He seemed to calm down a bit and he took us round the back and even brought some orange juice and biscuits. Things were going well. The others started digging up the nettles while I interrogated Mr Swan. (This is detective speak for getting people to answer questions.)

It turned out that he was an

inventor. Cool! I'd never met one before. But he had BIG PROBLEMS. Every time he had a new idea, it was stolen from the shed. As soon as he'd drawn out new plans, they disappeared. Was this why he had become so strange – he was worried about his work?

'I think it's one of the other inventors in the town,' he told me. 'Jealous of my success, that's what. Somebody who hasn't got ideas of his own, see.'

I had to agree that it made sense.

'I work in the shed so I've put padlocks on the door to try and keep him out,' he said. 'It's very important he doesn't get in before the competition.'

'Competition?'

'Yes. The Inventors' Competition. The plans have to be handed in on Monday. The prize is six thousand pounds.'

Wow! That was a lot of money.

I was getting some really valuable information, when Mr Swan suddenly had a violent outburst. A real tantrum. For no reason, he started yelling at Harry and Winston.

'STOP! MY ROSES!' he yelled. 'MY RHODODENDRON!'

He even started shaking his stick so we thought we'd better run for it.

Chapter 3

Back at my shed, I told the gang what I had found out.

'The fact is,' I said, 'Mr Swan is in a real state because there's a spy in the area.'

They were gobsmacked. A spy in our town! It was a real shock, I can tell you.

'What'th a thpy, Damian?'

'Spies go pinching other people's ideas,' I explained. 'It's big business. They make a fortune. They sell the ideas to companies. It's called Industrial Espionage.'

I could tell they were dead impressed by my knowledge of the criminal world.

'You mean thomebody's thpying on Mr Thwan?'

'Yes, Lavender. Somebody's spying on him.'

We all thought that was unfair. No wonder Mr Swan was desperate. No wonder he was liable to bouts of sudden temper. But I had a cunning plan to track down whoever was doing the spying. Once I had caught him, Mr Swan would get back to being a friendly old man and Lavender would be happy again.

Early on in my career, I had noticed that there were certain kinds of people who are crooks for sure.

These are the signs:

Criminal Type Number One: people with eyes close together.

Criminal Type Number Two: people with beards – especially black ones and usually on men.

My plan was to walk up and down Water Lane (in disguise, of course) looking for Criminal Types. This way I would prevent Mr Swan's spy from entering his garden and breaking into the shed. I would be there to stop him.

The only trouble was that Mum had other ideas. She was catering for a big party that afternoon. Bad luck! She wanted me to go with her.

'It's at the Town Hall and starts at four o'clock,' she told me. 'I'll have to leave at two to give me time to put the food on the tables.'

I tried to get out of it.

'You go, Mum. I'll stay here.'

It was no good. She shook her head. 'I don't think so, Damian. I am not leaving you at home – again. I don't know what would happen. No. You'll have to come with me.'

This was a blow. You see, when spies are in the area, you have to act quickly.

I protested. 'You don't like me going with you when you're working. You say I always get into trouble.'

'You usually do, Damian. But you can stay in the kitchen. You can't get up to much there, can you?'

I tried everything but nothing

worked. Mum insisted I had a shower and put clean clothes on – *that's how serious she was.*

Urgent action was called for. The rest of the Detective Team had to be alerted. I needed to speak to Tod and give him the news.

I turned the shower on so Mum would think I was in the bathroom. Then I went into her bedroom to use the phone.

'Tod,' I said. 'We've got an emergency. I can't work on the Spy Case this afternoon. I've got to go and help Mum at the Town Hall. She can't manage without me. You know how it is.'

Tod understood. He had a mum of his own and he knew all about helping out when she couldn't cope. Like when his bedroom needed tidying and when the rabbit's cage needed cleaning out. He sometimes had to help her out then.

'What do you want me to do, Damian?'

I explained that I had divided the area around Water Lane into three parts: one for Harry, one for Winston and his dog Curly and one for Tod and Lavender. They were only beginner detectives – I couldn't expect them to patrol a big area.

'All you have to do is to walk around your own bit of Water Lane, keeping an eye open for anyone who looks like a spy.'

'Sounds simple,' he said.

'Ring the others, Tod, and tell them. Don't forget your notebook and wear a disguise.'

'OK,' he said. 'And I'll take Thumper with me.'

This was good thinking because Thumper could smell a crook at a hundred metres. I had smashed the crime ring at the dog show only two weeks earlier and Thumper had been brilliant.

That done, I went back to the
bathroom where the shower was still
running. Unfortunately, the soap had
blocked the drain hole and water was
pouring out of the cubicle onto the
floor. I stayed cool and, just to be
helpful, I grabbed a couple of things to
mop up the water.

How was I to know that Mum had
intended to wear that sweater at the
party? It didn't look all that special to
me. She didn't have to shout at me,
did she? Sometimes, I don't think I'm
appreciated in our house.

Chapter 4

As I climbed into Mum's van, I felt depressed. I was leaving the gang to do important work while I was going to be stuck in a kitchen – probably doing the washing-up. This was bad news.

By the time we set off, Mum had got over her sulk about the sweater. In fact, she seemed quite cheerful. 'This should be an interesting party, Damian,' she said.

I was too miserable to reply. Nothing in the Town Hall on a Saturday afternoon could interest me.

But then she said, 'The party's for all the inventors in the area.'

'Inventors?'

Now I was interested.

'Yes. Their club's called Inventors Anonymous.'

'What's Anonymous mean?'

'It means keeping your name secret.'

My spine began to tingle. Why should anyone want to keep their name secret? Suspicious or what? They must be up to no good.

'They meet once a month,' said Mum, unaware of the vital information she was giving me, 'and they bring their latest inventions. If you're good – *really good, Damian* – I'll ask if you can look at them.'

Would I be good? I'd be an angel if it meant I could get to meet the inventors.

26

For the rest of the ride I felt quite excited. I even began to feel sorry for the other kids. They would be pounding the streets looking for spies when all the time the spy would probably be at the party.

The Town Hall was a massive old building. We parked round the back and started to unload the van.

'Don't touch a thing,' said Mum. 'I'll carry the food. Just follow me.'

Mum worries about her gateaux and stuff. She says I'm not to be trusted. She says I don't concentrate – but that can't be right. I've only tripped up a couple of times. Uneven pavements. Not my fault.

We went down twisty corridors with stone floors until we reached the kitchen which was big and old and smelled of cooked cabbage.

'You wait here, Damian, while I'll go back to get the rest of the things. *And don't move!*'

It was a long way back to the van. Mum would be ten minutes at least. And the smell was making me feel faint. I needed to get a breath of fresh air.

I sneaked down the passage towards the front of the Town Hall where I noticed that the floor was covered in red carpet. (A detective has to be observant.) I knew that red carpet meant 'important bits'.

Unfortunately, just as I had entered this interesting area, a large man in a black suit stepped out and blocked my way.

'Now, young man, where are you off to?'

Quick as a flash I said, 'I'm looking for Inventors Anonymous.'

He bent over, peered down at me and scratched his chin.

'A bit young for an inventor, aren't you?'

What a nerve.

'As a matter of fact,' I said, keeping my cool, 'I'm the youngest inventor in the area.'

He shook his head. 'I thought the youngest one was Peter Parker. He's a genius and only sixteen. Are you Peter Parker?'

I pulled myself up to my full height. 'I won't reveal my name. Don't you know that the club is called Inventors Anonymous? We keep our names secret.'

That fixed him.

'I'm sorry,' he said, looking embarrassed. 'Let me show you to the party room.'

He took me across to a large oak

30

door and pushed it open.

'Excuse me, gentlemen . . . and . . . er . . . lady, I believe I have one of your members here.'

Everyone in the room turned to look at me. There were five men and a woman. They all had beards (Criminal Type Number Two), except the woman – but I noticed that she had eyes that were pretty close together (Criminal Type Number One). In my experience, this meant that any one of them could be Mr Swan's spy. What was I going to do?

A tall man with a shaggy, black beard came over. 'Well, young man. And who might you be?' he asked but I noticed he didn't tell me his name.

I stuffed my hands in my pocket and looked down at the floor. My lips were sealed. I was determined not to give away my real identity.

But Black Beard didn't give up. He kept trying to make me talk. 'Come on, son. What's your name?'

The heat was on. The other inventors gathered round grinning at me in a spooky kind of way, trying to make me speak.

Luckily the door opened just then and everybody turned round to look.

'Ah, Peter, it's you,' Black Beard called out as a teenage boy walked in. At once I guessed that he must be the genius, Peter Parker. At least he didn't have a beard. He looked quite normal except for his very large glasses.

I scribbled his name on a piece of

paper. This information might be
useful later. Who knows – this might
be Criminal Type Number Three:
people wearing large glasses. I would
wait and see if he behaved
suspiciously.

'We've got a new member here,
Peter,' Black Beard said, pointing to
me. 'But he won't tell us his name.
Can you persuade him?'

On hearing these words, I backed up against a wall, afraid that he was might use violence to make me talk. I've seen thugs torture people in films on the telly just so they'll spill the beans. I didn't want it to happen to me.

'Stay away,' I yelled. 'I'll call the police.'

'We only asked your name.'

'Why do you need to know my name?'

'We just . . .'

'I won't tell you. I'll call Inspector Crockitt if you touch me. HELP! HELP! HELP!'

I knew if I yelled loud enough someone would come to my rescue.

In seconds, the door burst open and Mum rushed into the room.

Chapter 5

It turned out that when Mum explained the word 'anonymous' she had got it wrong – sort of. The inventors were not 'anonymous' at all.

When I told them, they all laughed.

'No, we don't keep our names secret. That's just the name of our club.'

Typical of a grown-up to get a kid into trouble, I thought.

Mum was not very pleased. I expect she felt embarrassed at making a mistake. She tried to blame me as usual.

'You shouldn't be here at all, Damian,' she said and her face turned bright red. 'You promised to stay in the kitchen.'

'Now, now,' said Black Beard (who told me his name was Albert Swindles), 'I expect the boy was just looking for a bit of adventure. Let him stay with us while you're seeing to the food. He can look at our inventions. He won't come to any harm here.'

Mum tried to protest. She liked to keep an eye on me, she said. But Albert Swindles persuaded her to let me stay. I wrote his name on the paper and put:

DEFFINITLY NOT A CRIMINLE TYPE EVEN IF HE HAS A BEERD.

'Peter will look after him,' he said. 'He's brilliant, you know. He's top student in his class.'

Mum is impressed by this kind of thing. 'Perhaps he can show Damian how important it is to work hard at school,' she said.

I just smiled and nodded. It's the only thing to do when grown-ups talk like that.

Once Mum had gone, I got down to serious detective work. After all, I was here to try and track down Mr Swan's spy. Which of these inventors might have stolen his ideas? I had another cunning plan. I would talk to each of them and try and trick them into revealing their criminal ways.

I soon got rid of Peter. He was only interested in setting up his Automatic Egg Boiling Machine – which is a crazy idea if you ask me. Everybody knows how to boil an egg. Even Mum.

I walked around the room with my

piece of paper ready to take notes. I tried to interview everybody but I noticed that they all avoided answering my questions. They said things like: 'I'm busy,' or 'I've got a lot to do,' or 'Just leave me alone.' Suspicious, I thought. The only one who would speak to me was the woman with close-together eyes. She had finished putting up her Lemonade Maker which looked very good. (I asked for a sample but I wasn't allowed.)

'Do you know Mr Swan?' I asked.

She shook her head. 'He used to come to our meetings but he stopped some months ago.'

I scribbled down this interesting fact. I knew I was onto something. 'Why did he stop coming?'

She blushed and looked kind of flustered. 'Well, he became a little . . . strange. He thought people were stealing his ideas.'

'And were they?'

She blushed even more. 'Of course not,' she said. But was she telling the truth? That's what I wanted to know.

Just as I was getting somewhere with my investigation, Mum came in with a trolley full of food and set it out on a huge table. Everybody rushed to grab a plate but I managed to get to the front of the queue.

'Damian!' Mum hissed. 'The food isn't for you. You're not an inventor.'

But Albert Swindles very kindly said

that I looked hungry and needed
feeding up. He insisted that I helped
myself. So, just to be polite, I loaded
my plate with sausage rolls and ham
sandwiches and crisps and my
favourite chocolate gateau.

I went to sit over by the window and
later Peter Parker came to sit next to
me. I even offered to finish off his
sandwiches as he didn't seem all that
hungry.

'You have them,' he said and handed me the plate. I noticed he was frowning as he stared at a large piece of paper he had pulled from his pocket.

'Is that the plan of your next invention?'

'It's not finished yet,' he said. 'I've only got another day to get it right before the competition.'

'Competition?' I said.

'The Inventors' Competition. The prize is £6,000.'

I almost choked on the last egg and cress sandwich. My detective's brain was racing.

Now I knew for certain that I had discovered Mr Swan's spy.

Chapter 6

When I got home that night, I rang
Tod and the other kids in the
Detective School.

'I have serious news,' I said. 'Come
round to the shed tomorrow. 10 sharp.
Bring your notebooks.'

The next morning, everybody
(except Harry) wanted to tell me how
they had got on the day before.

'We got vewy wet, Damian,' said Lavender. 'Hawwy had to go home. He couldn't thtop thneezing.'

I was surprised that Harry – who was bigger than any of us – had gone down with a cold. He must have forgotten to take his mac. A good memory is essential for a detective.

'We worked really hard,' said Tod. 'We saw a man with a beard in Mr Swan's street.'

'Cwiminal Type Number Two, Damian,' said Lavender, bouncing up and down.

'I know,' I said.

'And we followed him up to Mr Swan's door,' said Winston. 'We guessed he was going to break in so we tried to stop him. At least Thumper did.'

'Good man!'

'Not really. Our spy turned out to be the postman.'

I could see they had a lot to learn.

'He thed he'd weport uth to the poweece,' said Lavender.

'My mum'll go spare if the police come after me,' said Winston. 'So we've decided we don't want to do any more detective work. It's too dangerous.'

'Wait!' I said. 'I've got something to tell you. I've found the spy who stole Mr Swan's plans.'

Then I told them about Peter Parker – but it didn't make any difference. They didn't want to be involved. I supposed they were scared of mixing with criminals.

From then on, if I was going to catch Peter Parker, I was going to have to do it alone.

'There is one thing,' I said.

'What?'

'I need to borrow a tent.'

'Why do you need a tent?'

'Today is the last day before the plans have to be handed in for the competition. Peter Parker will break into Mr Swan's shed tonight, for sure. I have to be there – in hiding. And I need a tent.'

'Oh, Damian. You are bwave,' said Lavender. 'You can have my tent. It'th ever tho thweet. It'th got faiwieth all over it.'

I was horrified. Hiding out in a girlie tent covered in fairies was not the right image for a detective. But nobody else had one so what could I do?

My plan was this. Later on that night, I would climb out of my bedroom window and slip across to Mr Swan's house where I would lie in wait. That way, I would catch Peter Parker red-handed.

Chapter 7

I was pretending to watch TV with Mum but I was really thinking about my plan to catch Mr Swan's spy. I had to go to bed as soon as possible because it was getting dark. My detective's instinct told me that Peter Parker would strike soon under cover of darkness. So I started to yawn.

'You look tired, Damian,' said Mum.

'I think I'll have an early night. I've got to be up early for school tomorrow.' This didn't usually bother

me but I didn't know what else to say.

'Have you done your homework?'

I sighed. Why is Mum so keen on homework? I use my brains in other ways.

'That Peter Parker is a clever boy,' she said. 'He must work very hard at school.'

I couldn't tell her the truth, of course. I couldn't tell her he was a spy who stole other people's ideas. I just said, 'Some people are not what they seem to be, Mum.'

She gave me one of her funny looks and turned the telly up. 'Goodnight, love.'

I raced upstairs and played around in the bathroom for a few minutes. I wanted her to think everything was normal. Then I went into my bedroom and changed into a pair of dark jeans, a black sweatshirt and a baseball cap. It is essential to be invisible when working at night. Then I used a black

felt pen to colour my face. This took
ages but the effect was stunning. Only
my eyeballs were showing up white. I
soon fixed that by putting on my
shades. Perfect – although it might be
hard to see where I was going in the
dark.

By eight o'clock, I knew I had to
leave or I could be too late to catch the
spy. I pushed the window open,
climbed out onto the roof of the
kitchen and jumped down.

As I headed for Water Lane, it began to rain. I pulled my cap down to stop the ink running off my face and, once I got to Mr Swan's house, I quickly set up Lavender's tent in the front garden. I put it next to the gate near the low stone wall. Nobody would notice it as they walked down the lane – especially Peter Parker. I broke a few branches off some bushes and heaped them on the tent. The camouflage was brilliant. Nobody would know I was there.

I crawled inside out of the rain and waited.

Lavender's tent was a bit small and my feet stuck out at the end. But, with the branches on top, I was quite cosy and I closed my eyes. No need to keep a lookout. I would listen for Mr Swan's spy. I have excellent hearing.

That was when the unexpected happened. I was lying there near the gate when an elephant landed on top of me.

'AAAAHHHHGGG! HELP!' I yelled. I couldn't get up. I was squashed flat by its great weight. I could hardly breathe.

The elephant screamed. 'OOOOOOHHHHHH NO!' Quick as a flash, I realised that elephants don't speak. It must be Peter Parker! I could feel him struggling – but he couldn't get up. Some of the branches I had cunningly arranged on the tent were very prickly and he was finding it difficult to move. Unfortunately, so was I!

Using my fiercest voice, I shouted, 'DON'T THINK YOU CAN GET AWAY WITH THIS. YOU'VE BEEN CAUGHT RED-HANDED!'

'THAT'S WHAT YOU THINK!' he shouted back and suddenly I felt the weight of the Master Spy lift off my stomach. He had got himself free and he was going to escape.

Chapter 8

Just at that moment, I heard two cars pull up. One had a blue flashing light.

I struggled out of the tent and saw a shocking sight. Two policemen had arrived and were holding Albert Swindles! It was obvious that they had made a stupid mistake and had let Peter Parker get away.

'Why are you arresting him?' I said, pulling the foliage off my sweatshirt.

The policeman looked down at me as if I was an alien beamed down from outer space. 'I don't know what you're doing here, young man, but the owner of this house rang to say there was a disturbance in his garden.'

I understood, of course. Mr Swan was not to know I was tracking down a criminal.

'But you've got the wrong man,' I said. 'The real culprit has run off. This is Albert Swindles, the chairman of Inventors Anonymous? I shall speak to Inspector Crockitt about this.'

'You'll do no such thing, Damian!' I looked round to see Mum climbing out of her van with Lavender and Tod.

'Oh, Damian,' said Lavender as she ran towards me and flung her arms round my waist. 'We were vewy fwitened when your mum wang up and thed you weren't in your bed.'

'She was really worried,' said Tod. 'We had to tell her where you were.

Sorry, Damian.'

I understood. After all, they weren't trained in the art of keeping secrets.

Before Mum could have another go at me, Mr Swan came out of the house in his dressing gown and Tod's gran came from next door and most of the neighbours arrived about the same time. They seemed really angry about the disturbance.

Mr Swan was waving his stick at the police. 'About time,' he said. 'I dialled

999 ten minutes ago. Where have you been? Can't have hooligans camping out in my garden. What are things coming to?'

Then ANOTHER police car arrived. Three members of the local police jumped out.

'Missing child,' one called out. 'Have you found him then?'

Mum pointed to me. I was insulted. A missing child? Who could think that I, Damian Drooth, Master Detective and Spycatcher, could be a missing child?

I was standing in the middle of this noisy crowd, waiting to explain what I had been doing, when I noticed a vital clue. Albert Swindles had something poking out of his pocket. It could only be Mr Swan's plans.

Had my first guess about Albert Swindles been right after all? (He did have a beard – Criminal Type Number Two). At the party on Saturday, he had been clever enough to cover up his unlawful activities by being extra friendly towards me. He had fooled me for a time – but not for long.

There were a lot of people and a lot of shouting and nobody seemed to want to hear my side of the story. Then another police car arrived – which I thought was a waste of taxpayers' money – and out stepped Inspector Crockitt.

'What's this about a riot?' he said to one of the officers. 'What's going on?'

Then he spotted me.

'DAMIAN!' he said.

I smiled and waved at him. I know Inspector Crockitt very well. He regards me as an asset to the fight against crime.

'What are you up to this time?' he said. He was obviously keen to get all the information he could.

I explained about Mr Swan's spy. 'He must have been round the back, breaking into the shed while I was putting up my tent. He tripped over it on his way out . . .' Then I pulled the paper from Albert Swindles's pocket

and held it up for all to see.
'. . . AFTER HE'D GOT WHAT HE
CAME FOR.'

Everyone gasped. Mr Swan couldn't
believe his eyes. He grabbed the paper
and unfolded it. 'These are the plans
for my latest invention,' he said.
'Albert Swindles has probably been
stealing my ideas for months.' Then he
placed his hand on my shoulder. 'This
boy deserves a reward. He's better
than you lot rolled up in one. He is a
genius.'

Chapter 9

That is where the story ends. Except
to tell you that Mr Swan came second
in the Inventors' Competition and won
£3,000. (Peter Parker won first prize,
but we won't go into that.) He spent
some of the money on new roses and a
rhododendron and got someone in to
smarten up his garden.

When he was presented with his
prize, he took me along as his guest.
'You deserve it, Damian,' he said.

Mr Swan had to go up on a stage and give a speech. We were all expecting him to say, 'Thank you very much for the prize,' but he didn't. What he did say was a bit of a shock. 'The police in this town are rubbish,' he said. 'If you ask me, they couldn't find out Who Killed Cock Robin.'

Everyone laughed except Inspector Crockitt, who was sitting on the platform next to the Mayor. He didn't even titter.

'If you've got any problems,' Mr Swan continued, 'you should go and ask Damian Drooth. He'll solve 'em for you. The boy is brilliant.'

The audience cheered and wouldn't stop until I went up onto the stage. I didn't want to but when you're famous you have to do these things.

'You are a hewo, Damian,' said
Lavender, later. 'Mr Thwan ith hith
thweet old thelf again.'

'Back to biscuits and orange juice?'

'Yeth, Damian. Bithkits and owinge
jooth, thankth to you!'